Denying *The Stylus*
Brian D. Campbell

Printed in the United States of America
First Printing, 2020

ISBN 978-1-7329161-5-9 (Paperback)
ISBN 978-1-7329161-6-6 (Mobi eBook)

Red Cliff Press
PO Box 371
New Boston, NH 03070

Dedicated to Richard and Christine Campbell

My strength, my determination,
and my undeniable spirit.

Chapter 1
Pancake Day

Smiles and giggles filled the halls of Eastern State Hospital, on the outskirts of Williamsburg, Virginia. It was Friday morning and the patients were up and about in a blissful flurry.

The buzz had nothing to do with the coming weekend. Weekdays and weekends shared the same tedium for those of us who lived at Eastern. Friday was Pancake Day. And though the air was telling, with the thick and rich smell of maple syrup, I'd been gleefully reminded of the occasion four times before making it to my assigned table in the cafeteria.

"Tristan, let's go. Hurry. It's Pancake Day!"

Surely, no place on Earth was ever home to as many full-grown adults, overjoyed about another Friday-morning pancake breakfast than Eastern—the nation's oldest psychiatric hospital.

The original institution, constructed in downtown Williamsburg in 1773, had become a museum that many believed to be haunted by tormented souls of the past, when the place was known as the Eastern Lunatic Asylum.

By 1970, twelve years before my birth, the relocation to the more spacious site, at Dunbar Farm, outside of town, was complete.

There'd never been much for me to get excited about at Eastern, and I often felt envious of my fellow patients' repeated delight for things like Pancake Day, which could only be topped by Movie Night, occurring each and every Wednesday.

On that particular Pancake Day, I was feeling a rare bit of excitement, however, but it had nothing to do with the breakfast menu. I was expecting company. The very young and talented Mr. Ethan Alstead, writer for *Temporal Magazine*, had scheduled a visit to interview me.

I'd had several inquisitive visitors over the years, all with hopes of telling the world the bizarre story of why one the nation's most renowned scientists and inventors checked himself into a mental institution with no signs or prior history of illness, and remained there for years without being required to do so. They all hoped to be the first to get to the truth. They all failed.

Still, they kept coming, one after another for years, and I played along, but I never gave them what they wanted. None of them were worthy of it. And even if they were, it was too soon to share it. I couldn't risk telling the truth.

They published their interviews nevertheless—spun wild and speculative tales, and people believed some, dismissed others, and eventually forgot about all of them. And eventually, they forgot about me, too, which had been a blessing.

But then, after several lonely years had passed, young Ethan wrote me a letter. After reading the well-worded communication, to ease my interminable boredom, I decided to consume everything the young man had ever written, which only amounted to a failed novel and a handful of delightful articles published in *Temporal Magazine*.

I'd read his novel seven times. There was something beautiful about his story, though I was one of the rare few to have actually discovered it.

I'd come to admire Ethan, and we exchanged correspondence for weeks. He seemed worthy enough to share my story with the world. I'd hoped, if I was lucky, and if enough time had passed, I'd be able to finally confess the truth without gaining too much attention.

Hopefully, those who were ultimately responsible for my being at Eastern would believe as I did—that the truth was so wild, no one would ever believe it. And then I could live out my days there, in peace, with a clear conscience.

Hopefully, I could tell the world that I was in fact responsible for the death of one of America's favorite authors.

I killed Edgar Allen Poe.

Chapter 2
Mad Scientist

A generous amount of freedom had been granted to me to roam the grounds of Eastern. Most days, if I wasn't in my room reading from my own personal library, which contained every book I had ever asked for, I could be found outside working in one of the many gardens on campus.

The head gardener had given me a key to the tool shed, without objection from staff. Dr. Monroe, director of the facility, and my own personal psychiatrist, even suggested a wage be given for my efforts. An offer I declined, of course.

While I waited patiently for my visit with Ethan Alstead, however, I sat in the media room, daydreaming in front of a television that I paid absolutely no attention to, rehearsing answers to questions I knew he would ask, and others I'd hoped he might.

"Tristan, are you OK, man? You're talking to yourself. And your foot is tapping to the beat of something other than *The Talk*. Are you really watching that, T? Doesn't seem like something you'd be into."

I smiled and waved at Alex—the orderly who had been with me for all my years at Eastern, and my best friend. He gave a chuckle and moved on. "You mad scientists are all the same."

Alex was the only one who ever called me a mad scientist. I liked it. I liked Alex, a lot. Alex never lied to me, and he never looked at me the way everyone who works at Eastern looks at everyone who lives at Eastern. Alex was a good man—a good friend. Alex was my only friend.

Mad scientist? Maybe. Before I had come to be at Eastern, I was one of the top physicists in the country—perhaps the world. At twenty-four, just a few years out of MIT, I led a team of extremely talented individuals, working for the Department of Defense in Pottsville, Pennsylvania. We were a think tank for the government. Our job was to make the impossible possible. And we were very good at our job.

Science was in my blood. My father, an astrophysicist, retired from the Air Force and passed on an offer to work at NASA to become a high-school Physics teacher back home in Baltimore. Both of his parents were Physics professors at Johns Hopkins.

The work I'd done in Pottsville is what eventually brought me to Eastern. Some speculated that I'd cracked under the pressure—a common hazard for someone working at such a high profile job in the DoD. But I didn't crack at all. My team was exceptionally successful, and we enjoyed our work.

The problem was, we were too successful. I had, in fact, accomplished the impossible. Well, at least what was once believed to be impossible. A horrible, and unintended consequence of my success, proved to be unbearable, and that is what left me no choice but to check myself into Eastern State Hospital.

I wasn't forced to give up my position at the DoD, but I refused to go back to work, on principle. And to mitigate the damage my story could have caused, if I had decided to share it, I was forced to stay here, indefinitely.

If I remained at Eastern, no harm would ever come to me. If I chose to leave, but not return to work, I would undoubtedly be executed. It was conceivable that those with a vested interest in my remaining at Eastern would even attempt to erase my existence completely. Of course, they didn't understand that an actual erasure of my existence wasn't at all possible.

For my crime, I had accepted this fate. And though I could have gone back to my previous life at any time, if I agreed to spend the rest of it telling lies, I refused. I deemed that I could never be free. Living a lie is as much a prison as living at Eastern. I also strongly held that there had to be punishment for what I had denied the world. I had to be held accountable. And since no court could ever convict me for my offenses, I did it myself.

I was perfectly sane. I knew that, and Dr. Monroe knew it as well, though he would never have admitted it.

There I was, at Eastern, and there I intended to remain for the rest of my life.

Chapter 3
Finally, Someone Worthy

E than Alstead looked exactly as I'd imagined him—young, handsome, and clean cut. He was a polite, well-mannered, and well-spoken young man.

"It's a pleasure to meet you, Mr. *We are.*"

"The pleasure is mine, Mr. Alstead, but it's pronounced *wear*. As in, 'You *wear* a wonderful smile on your face.' But please, call me Tristan."

We shook hands, determined mutually, to proceed on a first-name-basis, and got straight to work.

The young man looked away a few times during his initial questioning, with perhaps a hint of an eye roll, and a forced exhale. I could tell he was trying—he was indeed polite—but he couldn't hide his frustration.

"Let me assure you, Ethan, you're not the first reporter to come and visit me who believed they were wasting their time. But I think after we're done here, you'll be the first to completely change your impression of me, and my story. I intend to give you something I never gave the others. I intend to give you the full truth. And if we do this right, if we trust and believe one another, this article could prove to be the break you've long been searching for."

"I'm sorry about that. It won't happen again. Hospitals just make me nervous. I'll get it together. We agreed to seven additional one-hour sessions after today, and I want us to be completely open and honest with each other. I'm anxious to hear your story, and share it with our readers."

"There's nothing to be nervous about. In fact, most of the patients here would prove to be the most sincere individuals you've ever met. I find them to be of the highest quality people I've ever had the joy of being around. If you show them love and respect, they show it back to you, in earnest."

His tone and demeanor improved, thankfully. I had begun, for a moment, to believe he wasn't worthy of my story. But he quickly reassured me.

I don't remember many of the barrage of initial questions from our first session, and I can't say if I answered most of them honestly. I'd like to think I did, but I was engrossed in studying Ethan and lost in thought. Was he being sincere? Was he interested? Was he worthy?

He finally brought me to my senses by repeating one of his questions.

"Tristan? I work for the newly created *Temporal Magazine*. You must understand our obvious interest in your story? Our focus has been all things related to time. All of the reports I've read about you say you claimed to have discovered the secret to time travel, and you were close to proving it. What happened ten years ago? How did you end up here?"

"Now that's the one question that everyone has asked me from the beginning. How did I end up here? It's the only question that matters, isn't it?"

Ethan's brow lowered, and he looked away.

"Oh you haven't offended me, don't worry. You had to ask that question, you had no choice, really. What about you, Ethan Alstead, author of one of my favorite books—and I am a voracious reader, by the way—how did you end up here? Why are you troubling yourself with interviewing a man in an insane asylum that the rest of the world has long forgotten?"

"You've read my book?"

The look of astonishment on his face was enjoyable, but it quickly faded and changed to a look of ignominy.

Ethan continued, "Well, since almost no one else has, I was left with no other choice but to look for work that comes with a paycheck. And I wanted to keep writing, so, thanks to a close relationship with an editor at *Temporal*, I got the only writing job I could find."

"That's not a good enough answer. You have obvious talent. You're an excellent writer, and when I read your book, I could tell you knew it. You could have had success on your own, if you kept trying. So, why are you here? Dig deeper before you answer."

Ethan looked up at the ceiling and took a deep breath. Would I get the truth? Does he know what the truth is?

"I have an attitude problem. Two different editors and my agent told me if I made simple adjustments to my style and focused more on what the reader wanted, I could gain more popularity and actually sell books. But I was young, inexperienced, and arrogant. I wrote my second novel, which remains unpublished, the same way I wrote my first. It was probably more contrary to what they were suggesting, just because— well, screw them, that's why."

Honesty. Pure, angry honesty. It was perfect. He was perfect.

"So, that's why I'm here. Now, can you tell me why you're here?

"Now you deserve an honest answer, Ethan. You mentioned time travel. I not only discovered the secrets of time travel, and proved them, as those articles you mentioned suggest, while working for the Department of Defense, I applied them. I traveled in time. On my initial voyage, I set out to meet one of my favorite figures from the past. I needed to find a subtle way to show that I'd visited with him, and create documented, indisputable proof for my superiors that I had accomplished what many believed to be impossible."

"With all due respect, that's not a good enough answer. With a discovery like that, you should be one of the most celebrated scientists in history. I should have read about you in junior high school. So, I'll ask again. Why are you here?"

He had returned my own words in a clever fashion. And I couldn't tell if he believed me or not. I supposed, of course, that he didn't, but I had time to convince him.

He seemed more interested in me than the unnamed figure I went back to visit. I should have told him it was Edgar Allan Poe.

"You're right. There's more to it than that. As you can see, I'm not restricted in my movements here. I can come and go as I please. No one is watching me. One would assume I'm here of my own free will. But, as we'll discuss in our next several sessions, I had no choice but to come here. And I have no choice now, but to remain here."

I paused, to allow the young man to respond, but he just stared at me, indicating he wanted me to continue. Our time was nearly up.

"If we're to continue next week, and beyond, you'll need to return with an open mind. You're going to have to trust me, and you're going to have to stop being afraid of our surroundings. You're in far less danger here than you are out there, I assure you. As far as my safety goes, there's a fair chance that what I'm going to tell you over the next several weeks could result in an untimely end to my life. If you'll allow me, and hear me out till the end, I'll share a story with you that will resuscitate your career as a writer."

Chapter 4
A Terrible Cup of Coffee

My days at Eastern were still filled with the same dreadful monotony and routine that they had been for nearly ten years. But I had something to look forward to for the next seven Pancake Days. Mr. Ethan Alstead had seven more one-hour sessions left to complete his research and hopefully follow it with a brilliant article in *Temporal Magazine* that would share my confession with as broad an audience as possible.

On the Thursday before session number two, I walked the halls of Eastern and shared a "Hello, how are you?" and a smile with everyone I passed. My atypical-gleeful deportment caught the attention of my good friend, Alex.

"What's up, T? I don't know what's gotten into you, man, but I like it," Alex admitted.

"Do you have a minute, Alex? If you buy me a cup of coffee in the staff lounge, perhaps we can chat about it."

"I do indeed, sir. But before we do, let me remind you, for the millionth time, the world's worst coffee, served daily in the staff lounge, doesn't cost me a dime. Between you and me, they should pay us extra to drink it. I dunno, maybe some kinda hazard pay?"

I followed Alex into the staff lounge, another privilege I had been bestowed at Eastern that none of my fellow patients shared.

"I think I know why you're walking around here whistling classical tunes that no one's ever heard of. You have a visit scheduled tomorrow with the *Temporal* reporter. Am I right?" Alex inquired.

"As usual, you are correct."

"I don't get you, man. You've been toying with these reporters for years. They come in here all full of steam and excitement, hoping to break the news to the world about the mad scientist, and you size them up, deem them *unworthy,* and then send them home all disappointed and pissed off."

"Correct again, my friend."

"Well, now, here we are, years later. Ain't nobody come in here to interview you in forever but this guy from *Temporal*. But he's definitely not excited to see you. He had a look on his face like he'd rather be anywhere but here. Honestly, I think he was scared. Maybe afraid all the mental illness in here is something he's about to catch, like the flu? You know, *that guy*? That's the one you get excited about."

"You're three for three. You're on a roll, Alex."

"Is it because you haven't had a visitor, other than your father, for so long?"

"Oh, dear. Your hot streak is over, I'm afraid. And bringing up my father is a sure way to dampen my blissful disposition."

"Your father loves you. He hasn't missed a single visit in ten years. That's not something you oughta be upset about."

I couldn't argue that point, so I didn't try. Alex was only showing me how much he cared. He had no idea about my relationship with my father. And though I counted him my best friend, and he was, I didn't want to bring him into the labyrinth of emotion that existed between me and my father. So I didn't. I quickly changed the subject, like I had for years, every time Alex talked to me about my father.

"This reporter *is* different. He's afraid to be here, but I'll educate him. And yes, he's coming in like a reluctant seventh grader, forced to write a book report on *To Kill a Mockingbird.* But there's something special about him. He's gifted—loaded with talent that he's not currently employing. And even if he wasn't, he's got better timing than any of the others. Simply stated, now is the time to tell my story. Ethan Alstead is just lucky enough to be at the right place, at the right time."

I smiled at Alex and sipped my cup of terrible coffee. I wondered if he knew I was lying.

He gave me a smirk and tilted his head downward, to the right. He knew I was lying.

"Well, T. I gotta get back to work. You're welcome to finish your cup of coffee and let yourself out of here, if you want to. Oh, and don't think for a minute I believe any of that bullshit you just fed me either."

I took Alex up on his offer, and sat alone in the staff lounge for as long as it took to force down my coffee. Alex was always brutally honest with me. That pure honestly could only be found in my fellow patients at Eastern. Alex was a good friend. Alex was my only friend.

Chapter 5
The Rules of Time Travel

I had decided to take a brisk walk outside, after indulging in yet another pancake breakfast on the Friday of Ethan's second visit. I watched in amusement, making my way back inside to greet him, as he argued with the guard at the gate about the rules for bringing food into the facility for patients. It seemed young Mr. Alstead had coffee and pastries to share.

"Greetings, Ethan. I have to compliment you on your ability to negotiate a circumvention of the rules with Mr. Hendall, out front. You're the first person I've witnessed in ten long years to have success with such an endeavor."

The young reporter laughed and smiled warmly. I'd also noticed that on his way in, he stopped and had a pleasant conversation with Carol at the front desk, and gave anyone on his path a friendly greeting. This behavior was an impressive improvement from a week prior.

"It wasn't easy getting this stuff in here. That guy was tough, but I was able to sweet talk him. The apple turnover didn't hurt either."

"There's no shame in bribery, Mr. Alstead."

Ethan flashed another intoxicating smile. "I wanted to make a peace offering to you, and anyone around who's interested. I felt like we got off on the wrong foot last week."

"Your intentions are appreciated, but your timing is unfortunate. You see, today is Friday. That's a very popular day around here. Friday is Pancake Day, and most of us have celebrated that fact by eating enough pancakes to satisfy a pony, I'm afraid."

"Oh, well, hopefully they don't go to waste. I brought coffee too," he added.

"I'm sure they'll be gone before lunch time. And I've no doubt people will be singing your praises. Shall we get started?"

Ethan quickly pulled out his recorder and a note pad. "Absolutely. I'm anxious to talk more about time travel, and discover who you decided to meet from the past, but first I'd like to hear more about your life, leading up to your time at the Department of Defense."

"Fair enough," I answered blankly. I wanted to get to the good stuff, but suspected at some point we'd have to talk, at least a little, about my life.

"I grew up in Baltimore, Maryland. My father was an astrophysicist in the Air Force who was almost never home, until he retired from the military and became a Physics teacher at Central High School. My mother didn't work, but she was busy enough with me and my six older siblings."

Ethan was looking for something deeper. "Interesting. So, you grew up in a pretty normal household then?"

"Things were harder for my older siblings. We moved around a lot, due to my father's position in the Air Force, but by the time I was ten years old, he had begun his second career, teaching, and we finally settled down and planted roots. From age ten on, I'd say I had a fairly typical childhood."

Ethan pursed his lips. "You had a good relationship with your parents?"

"Perhaps we should invite Dr. Monroe to join us for the psych evaluation?" I offered to the young reporter.

Ethan's smile suddenly returned to his face. "No, that won't be necessary. I'm sorry if I've offended you. I just need to gather as much information as possible for the story."

"Of course," I returned. "Well, other than the fact that he's impossible to please—maybe a side effect of a distinguished military career, I had a normal relationship with my father."

"Had?" Ethan persisted. "I'm sorry, did you lose your father then?"

Well done, Ethan! "No, my father is very much alive. He visits me every week, still, after ten years. We get along well enough, though he insists I don't belong here, and refuses to accept any reasoning I offer. We spend his visiting hour arguing. And then he comes back a week later to have the same conversation all over again."

Ethan's eyes grew wide. He was pleased with himself, no denying it.

"Tell me more about how you came to work for the Department of Defense."

"I had achieved my PhD from MIT at the age of twenty. That, and a few wildly debated papers on the realities and conditions of time travel had caught their attention."

Ethan paused and scribbled notes on his notepad. I wondered if he'd attempt to get copies of my papers.

"So you left MIT, at the tender age of twenty, and accepted a job working for the government at the DoD?"

"That's correct. And, before my twenty-seventh birthday, I traveled in time to meet one of my favorite figures in American history. None other than the legendary Edgar Allan Poe," I nearly shouted. I couldn't possibly wait any longer.

"You met Edgar Allan Poe?"

Finally, the good stuff. "That's correct. I met with Poe in the year 1836, two years before he published his one and only complete novel…"

"You traveled from some basement in the Department of Defense in Washington D.C., to where? Baltimore or Boston in 1836, to meet with Poe?" Ethan interrupted.

"It doesn't quite work that way. You can't travel in time and over space simultaneously. My office was actually in Pottsville, Pennsylvania. And by mid-1836, Poe was living with his thirteen-year-old wife, and first cousin, Virginia Clemm, in Richmond, Virginia."

Ethan's expression grew blank, and I quickly realized how many objects I'd just lobbed at him to juggle with that answer.

"Let's just focus on time travel, for now," I offered. "On my maiden voyage, I had to set up my equipment in an existing military installation in Richmond that also existed in 1836, and open a portal to that specific location, in that specific time. I always traveled with an active military companion, who served as my security, and government babysitter. His duty was to protect me, brief and prepare his counterparts in the past, and report my every move back home to our superiors."

"Fascinating," was Ethan's only response.

"Once we opened the portal and made initial contact in 1836, our first objective was to establish communications, which would allow us to travel to prepared military installations during future trips. This would make it much simpler to proceed."

"Okay. You arrived in 1836, at some military installation. Your companion then explained your mission to the undoubtedly shocked people there, and eventually you worked out all the details for future visits to various locations in the past?"

"Exactly," I admitted. Well done again, Mr. Alstead.

"And then it was on to meet with Edgar Allan Poe?"

"Correct. My mission was to meet with Poe, and create some type of documented evidence that I was there."

"So you do something to alter the past, and then come back home to point out the difference you made?"

"Well, yes, but it's not quite that simple. Time travel is only possible because alternate realities exist on their own timeline for every possible outcome. There's an infinite number of possible outcomes from every point in time. When you travel in time, you're not actually moving back and forth on the same timeline. You're skipping to another reality, on another timeline, where your visit actually occurred. And the future outcome, after that point in time, proceeds toward the anticipated result. When you go back to the same timeline you left, it's entirely possible that whatever change you created never happened in your current reality."

"That's tricky," Ethan said with a unconvinced grin.

I ignored the skepticism and continued. "You can't always alter the past. At least not the past of your current reality—in most cases. And you can only travel backward, or forward to the point of your current existence, where your journey began. You can never move into a future that hasn't actually occurred yet."

"Kinda like using a DVR with a live show?" Ethan asked.

"Precisely, very impressive analogy, Ethan."

"So how could you ever prove you actually traveled in time?" Ethan inquired.

"With a little luck, and a few exceptions," I answered.

"Tell me about your meeting with Poe."

"That's all the time we have today, I'm afraid. But I'm eager to pick up there, next week."

Chapter 6
An Extraordinary Coincidence

Over five-hundred weeks had passed since I first arrived at Eastern, but none seemed to pass more slowly than the time between my second and third session with Ethan.

We had just begun to talk about my first visit with Poe, and it was time to stop. I couldn't sleep. I could hardly focus on reading, or working in the garden. My concentration for seven days had been fixed on remembering every detail of my time with Poe, so I could share it with Ethan. If I were to tell my story properly, I had to make sure I left nothing out.

I made myself comfortable in the small meeting room, near the front desk, where I had met with Ethan the week before, and waited.

"What's up, T?" Alex asked, interrupting my rehearsal for session three.

"I'm waiting for Mr. Alstead from *Temporal*."

"He's not gonna be here for another hour, man. You anxious or something?"

"We're at an important part of the story. I wanted to make certain I'm fully prepared to tell him what needs to be told."

"So this one's worthy?"

"Indeed."

Alex didn't say anything else, but he lingered in the doorway of the meeting room and stared into space, looking like he wanted to speak. He had a markedly sad expression on his face. He took a deep breath, looked down at the floor, and slowly waked away.

Alex's odd behavior was the first thing to break my concentration in seven days, but I continued on with my rehearsal for Ethan.

When Ethan finally arrived, once again with pastries I was too full to eat, I had expected to start right where we left off. It was time to talk about Poe.

"I understand you're eager to tell your story, but I have to be as thorough as possible, and collect as many relevant facts as I can. Please allow me to ask a few questions before we get there."

Ethan had burst my bubble, and I struggled to play along. He had successfully delivered the message that he was in charge of this interview, and if I didn't follow the rules, there would be no interview. I must admit, despite my disappointment, I respected him for that.

There were more questions about my state of mental health before checking into Eastern. Were there any issues at MIT? Did I have any problems at work, at the Department of Defense? Were there any disciplinary issues here at Eastern? I had to hand it to him—the man was quite thorough indeed.

"Okay, let's get back to your initial meeting with Poe," Ethan finally offered.

"This really is the most important part of my story. And in my opinion, it should have been enough to prove, beyond any doubt, that I had traveled to the past, created documentation that I was there, and safely returned to the present."

"But it wasn't?" Ethan asked.

"No, unfortunately it wasn't. At least not to my superiors at the DoD."

Ethan nodded with a smile. He still thought I was mad.

"Before my travel companion and I set out to meet with Poe, in 1836, we made several test jumps to the military installation in Richmond, at various times, to brief them and make future arrivals less confusing for them. However, as we moved from one time to another, and as I had predicted in my alternate timeline theory, no one ever knew we were coming. There were infinite realities, resulting in infinite timelines. We had to initiate contact each and every time, with a group of people, some of whom we had seen before, who were astonished to see us. My theory had been proven, but at great frustration. My travel companion had an idea to take a newspaper from one of our visits—a copy of *The Richmond Dispatch*, from 1884. The idea being, this would prove to someone at an earlier time that we were from the future, thus making our briefing period less arduous. It was a good idea, but it didn't work."

"So you traveled in time with your companion several times before actually meeting Poe?" Ethan asked.

"Yes, but that was only one part of our mission. We needed to establish documented proof. A copy of a newspaper wasn't enough, and none of our military base visits were actually recorded upon our return to our own timeline."

"How did you finally come up with something you thought would satisfy your bosses?"

"We decided to go ahead with the plan, and initiate contact with Poe. Can you imagine my excitement? I was finally going to meet one of my heroes. We jumped back to Richmond in 1836, to yet another briefing at the military installation, got a change of clothes to fit in with the times, and traveled to the Poe residence."

"So you just walked up and knocked on Edgar Allan Poe's door? Like a couple of Bible salesmen?"

I could feel Ethan's skepticism, but I ignored it and continued. "I suppose, yes, we did. And to my amazement, he greeted us with a smile and invited us in. We exchanged pleasantries, and introduced ourselves. He thought we were publishers or magazine editors, looking to offer him work. He'd achieved a bit of fame by then, but was still struggling financially. He hoped we were about to offer him his first big break."

"How did he handle the news that you were just some hyper-intelligent super fan from the future who invented a time machine in order to go back and meet your favorite author?"

I ignored the sarcasm and continued with my story. "He kept telling us about a novel he was working on— *The Narrative of Arthur Gordon Pym of Nantucket.* Are you familiar?"

"Yes, of course. It's about adventures at sea, lots of crazy tales."

"It was Poe's one and only complete novel. And my visit with him resulted in a grizzly contribution that eventually shocked literary historians. The novel includes the unfortunate fate of a real-life cabin boy named Richard Parker, who was a victim of cannibalism aboard an ill-fated yacht."

"Wait, I think I know that story," Ethan admitted.

"I believe you do. In 1884, Richard Parker was among a group of four sailors hired to deliver a yacht to a man in Australia. They ran into bad weather, and the yacht was sunk. The four were adrift on a lifeboat, and on the nineteenth day of their ordeal, a desperate decision was made by the other three sailors. Since Parker was the youngest, and he was already ill from drinking too much seawater, they would eat him in order to survive. The three remaining sailors were rescued five days later, with a hell of a story to tell."

"And there's a chapter in Poe's book that describes a similar scene?"

"Indeed there is. *The Narrative of Arthur Gordon Pym of Nantucket* was published in 1838—forty-six years before the real Richard Parker met his terrible end, and less than two years after my visit with Poe. In the novel, Pym was a stowaway on a whaling vessel called the *Grampus*. After a mutiny aboard the ship, a terrible storm, and an eventual overthrowing of the mutiny, Pym is left at sea with three other survivors—one of them named Richard Parker. The ship was badly damaged by the storm, with no mast, and they were unable to navigate. They were adrift, and faced starvation. Richard Parker had suggested that one of them should be killed and used as food so the others could survive. The four drew straws, and Parker lost."

"So you told Poe all about the story from 1884, and he put it in his novel?"

"Not directly, no. While attempting to explain to Poe that my companion and I were on a mission to travel in time and meet him, my companion pulled out the copy of *The Richmond Dispatch* he had been carrying with him as a form of proof. Poe convinced me to let him keep it, and the true story of Richard Parker happened to be printed on the paper."

"But that story was in Poe's novel before you traveled back in time to meet him."

"No, Ethan. It wasn't. I'd read that book more than once before ever meeting Poe. Richard Parker's story only appeared in the novel *after* the meeting took place. Upon my return, since Poe had mentioned the novel specifically during our visit, I went back to it and found the difference. I was able to get an archived copy of the paper I had left with Poe, and discovered the news story."

"But you said you can't change events on your own timeline. How were you able to change what was actually written in a novel?"

"I said in most cases. We'd also tried planting devices in remote parts of Virginia, at all the various times we'd visited. We'd buried them with time stamps and specific plaques on them, to retrieve upon our return home, but none of them were there when we returned. Not one device from any of the times we visited. But, Poe's novel had changed."

"Then you had your proof, right?"

"Unfortunately, I was the only person in the group that had ever actually read *The Narrative of Arthur Gordon Pym of Nantucket*. And since no copies without Richard Parker's story had ever existed, on our current timeline, I had no proof. And to the rest of the world, the novel had always included the Richard Parker story. My superiors dismissed my proof, and called it an extraordinary coincidence."

Chapter 7
Carl Sagan

My father and I never got along very well, because we were too much alike. At least that's what my mother used to say.

There were obvious similarities—we both excelled at science, we both devoted the early parts of our lives to our jobs, and ultimately we both chose to slow things down in the latter parts of our lives. He became a school teacher, and I checked into a mental health institution. I'd told that joke to him several times during his visits at Eastern, but never got a laugh from him. At least Alex thought it was funny.

Beyond those obvious similarities, there existed some vast differences. My father could be cold, emotionally. When I was very young, even when he was home, which wasn't often, he was a ghost. While he was home from work, he vanished into my parents' bedroom, and worked at a small table he'd used as a desk. The only time we heard from him was when he yelled at us to keep quiet.

I don't believe I'd ever heard the man utter the words "I love you" to me, my siblings, or even my mother. Hugs and kisses from dad were simply too much to hope for.

I'd recognized this as a young child, and despised it, which caused me to pour affection onto my mother at every opportunity. Any attempts to do the same with my brothers or sisters resulted in a pummeling.

It seemed my older siblings, none of whom had any passion for science, and none of whom had ever visited me at Eastern beyond my first two years as a patient, received the cold and distant emotional traits from my father. And I inherited his fervent love of science that superseded nearly all other pursuits.

Despite being emotionally absent for most of my childhood, my father managed to change just enough in my teenage years to build some form of a relationship with me. He recognized my aptitude for math and science, and we invented a code game together, using books and textbooks.

He would mark up a series of letters throughout whatever book I was engrossed in at the time, which could be decoded using various mathematical deciphers only he and I understood. I'd spend hours decoding the letters, which gave away clues to a location throughout the house, and sometimes even beyond our house, where he'd hid things like money, or a book he thought I'd be interested in. And usually, when it was a book, it contained a whole new code for me to work on.

We hardly spoke to each other. And when we did speak, with actual words, he'd push me. Nothing I'd accomplished seemed to please him—we argued constantly. But we'd spend hours speaking through code. That's how we communicated. That's how we formed our bond.

The bond, as well as the animosity, remained strong during my time at Eastern State Hospital. My father made the three hour drive, from Baltimore to Williamsburg, almost every week for ten years to visit with me. Even though we didn't have much to say, and often ended our visits with anger, he always came back to see me.

"Tristan. Your father's waiting for you in the meeting room. You should go see him."

The only time my friend ever called me by my actual name, was when my father was in the facility.

"I'm aware, Alex. I'm on my way to see him now."

I waited a few minutes longer, for no particular reason at all, and then made my way to the meeting room.

"Hello, Dad, how was your drive?"

"Tristan, thanks for coming down. I was beginning to wonder if I'd be spending the entire hour alone."

"I'm sorry. You know me and my busy schedule. I was reading Carl Sagan's *The Varieties of Scientific Experiment*, again."

"That showboating egoist? You'd be better off using the pages of that rag as toilet paper. *Carl Sagan*. Surely you have something better to do than waste your time reading that garbage—even in here."

My father hated Carl Sagan with more passion than he's ever felt for anything in his existence. He believed Sagan was using his scientific knowledge to become a celebrity, and not for its intended purpose—to leave the world a better place than how he'd found it. I'd made it a point to mention Sagan's name in at least one of every four visits with my father.

"If you miss science so much, why not get out of here and go back to work. I'm told there's still a place for you at MIT, if you want it."

"I believe we've just witnessed a new record, Father. Indeed, we have. Forty-five seconds into our hour, and you're already telling me I don't belong here. As if I could just get up and walk out as I please."

"Well, you could. And we're twenty minutes into the hour. You left me sitting here alone at least that long."

"My compliments to you. Way to make up for lost time."

"Why do you do this? I've spoken with your doctor, and I'm convinced there's nothing wrong with you. As far as I'm concerned, the only reason they haven't thrown your ass out of here is they're afraid to lose all the money the Department of Defense pumps into this place to keep you comfortable."

"To keep me here, Dad. The money is sent to keep me here."

"Oh don't give me any more of that baloney. I've read the nonsense they wrote about you in the papers. They claim you discovered time travel, but the government wants to use your so-called time machine as a weapon, so they forced you into this place and won't let you leave. It's bullshit."

Well, I'd never actually told any of them that much. They sort of took what little I gave them and ran with it. Wait until he reads Ethan's article.

"I'm afraid it's a bit more complicated than that. But you know I can't tell you anymore of the details," I told my father, for what had to be the one thousandth time.

"Of course it is. It's all so very complicated. If it wasn't complicated, you'd have to explain it all to your loving father."

And that was the closest thing to an "I love you" my father had ever given me.

"So, Dad. See you next week?"

"Yeah, you'll see me next week. And I'm not giving up. You can fight me every single time I come here if you want."

"I wouldn't have it any other way."

"Wouldn't you? If you really are into some trouble with the government, come home. Come back to me and your mother and we'll figure this out, together. We're willing to help you."

"I wish you could. I really do wish you could."

Chapter 8
Anonymous

My stomach growled ferociously in the meeting room. I'd done the unthinkable— I'd skipped breakfast on Pancake Day. Alex sent two different messengers, both fellow patients, to check on me to make sure I was awake and well.

"I'm perfectly fine. Please thank Alex for me, but I'm having breakfast with a visitor this morning."

"But Tristan. It's Pancake Day!"

"I'm fully aware, Max. Please tell Alex everything is fine. Go, and get your pancakes. Hurry, before they're all gone. I'm having something else for breakfast today, with a visitor."

At least I'd hoped I was. Ethan had been kind enough to bring pastries his last two visits, but I didn't have enough of an appetite to eat one, either time. A breach of etiquette I'd hoped to avoid during our fourth session together.

"Good morning, Tristan. How were your pancakes today?" Ethan inquired as he reached out to shake my hand.

My smile dropped immediately and my stomach gave an equally disappointed groan.

"Everything all right, Tristan? Is this a bad time?" my empty-handed visitor politely inquired.

I quickly came to my senses. "Everything is fine. I'm sorry. I just lost track of time. I didn't realize it was time for your visit already," I lied and managed a polite grin. I wondered if the cafeteria would be closed until lunch time. Of course it would.

"Excellent. And since I know how eager you are to tell your story, I'm not starting with any questions this time. Let's pick up right where we left off, okay? Last week you mentioned your bosses didn't believe you'd actually traveled in time after your first visit with Poe. What did you do next?"

"Well, let me clarify for you first. My bosses, or immediate supervisors at the Department of Defense, did actually believe my security companion and I had in fact jumped to a different time, on a different timeline. The issue was, we had failed to provide documented evidence for others in the DoD, who held higher positions in the chain of command."

"Fair enough. So, I'm guessing then, you made a second attempt?"

I'd paused at the question. Why wasn't Ethan more interested in the fact that I'd met with Edgar Allan Poe? Wasn't he curious about what Poe was like? Wasn't he curious about Virginia Clemm, or nineteenth-century Richmond, before the Civil War had changed everything forever? The obvious answer—he still didn't believe my story.

I took a deep breath and answered the question. "Yes, we made a second attempt to create some form of documented evidence. My immediate superior actually devised a plan, though I didn't believe it would work. I felt it would be insulting to Mr. Poe."

"This sounds interesting. What did they want you to do? Why did you believe it would insult Poe?"

"The plan was for me to convince Poe to write a poem, about a specific topic, with a specific title, that my team in the present knew had never existed. Poe would, of course, have to ensure that the poem be published, so we could find it when we returned to our regular timeline."

"Did you go through with it? Which poem? Why would this be an insult to Poe?"

"I did go through with it. The poem was titled *Epigram for Wall Street,* and it was published in 1845. That's the same year my companion and I returned to visit Poe for the second time. This time Poe and his positively lovely wife, Virginia Clemm, who had become terribly ill with tuberculosis, lived in New York—in Lower Manhattan, actually."

"Virginia Clemm? His thirteen year old cousin?"

"Yes indeed, his first cousin, but she was twenty-two by then. And by all accounts, she loved her husband. And Poe, though he did have a wandering eye, loved her back."

"So how did it go when you let Poe in on the plan to write a poem? Was he insulted?"

"It didn't go well at first. But I believe that may be more my fault. I had confronted him about the addition of Richard Parker in his novel, and he became quite defensive."

"I wondered about that. Did he think you were accusing him of plagiarism or something?"

"Perhaps. He did contest that the story of Richard Parker didn't exist when he read it in the paper we had given him, and therefore it was perfectly acceptable for him to write about."

Ethan just grinned at me. He nearly laughed.

"Nevertheless, I told him the change in his book actually made it to my timeline, and it wasn't there before we'd met. That didn't sit well with Poe. In 1844, a year before the visit we're discussing now, Poe published a short story called *A Tale of Ragged Mountains*. In that short story, Poe implied that time travel can't alter history because whatever the traveler does would have happened all along. Poe clearly didn't believe my visits, or anything we discussed during them, would actually alter history. And he was right, according to my own theory at least. Except, of course, for the Richard Parker story. How that story made it back to my timeline with my travel companion and I still mystified me."

"Tell me about the poem," Ethan requested.

"I explained to Mr. Poe that even though his novel had changed, I still needed his help to provide some documented evidence, for science, and for my superiors. I cautioned Mr. Poe that it should be subtle enough for the world to be blind to it. He reluctantly agreed to write the poem. He held firm to his belief that we couldn't possibly change history, no matter what we did. To be perfectly honest, I believed the same thing. Until I saw it with my own eyes on the pages of Poe's novel."

"How does the poem go?"

I recited *Epigram for Wall Street* for Ethan, from memory.

> I'll tell you a plan for gaining wealth,
> Better than banking, trade or leases—
> Take a bank note and fold it up,
> And then you will find your money in creases!
> This wonderful plan, without danger or loss,
> Keeps your cash in your hands, where nothing can
>   trouble it;
> And every time that you fold it across,
> 'Tis as plain as the light of the day that you double it!

"I've never heard of that one," Ethan admitted.

"It's not a particularly popular poem. And to finally answer your question about this plan being insulting to Mr. Poe—no, he wasn't insulted by the suggestion. To me though, it just seemed like nothing he'd ever written before. It didn't fit. Still, he wrote it. And though he didn't like it, in fact I'm sure he hated it, before I left he promised me he'd have it published. And he kept his word."

"So you finally had your proof?"

"Most of us believed so. We'd also left markers all around New York, like we did in Richmond in 1836. And once again, none of those markers were found when we returned to our present timeline."

"But the poem, which your team named, was published in 1845. That should have amazed everyone."

"Poe didn't put his name to the poem," I replied quietly. "It was published anonymously. Perhaps because he hated it, or he felt it wasn't his, even though he was only given a title and a theme. The words were all his. The poem was credited to Poe, but there was no proof in history that he was the one who'd actually written it."

"Oh come on! That poem didn't exist when you left your current time, and then it appeared when you returned. That's proof, no matter who wrote it," Ethan insisted.

"To everyone on my team, it was an amazing breakthrough. We celebrated it. Well, my team celebrated. I was fascinated by the fact that only changes to Poe's work, influenced by my visits, had shown up on our timeline. Why nothing else? The placement of the markers? Our visits to various military installations? All of those other things appeared to have never happened when we went back. I was too busy to celebrate. I had a puzzle to solve, and I had no idea how to solve it."

Ethan's tone had softened. "They didn't believe you again? Another coincidence?"

I was touched by Ethan's tender tone. Had he begun to believe me? Or did he feel sorry for me?

"Some believed me. Others insisted we didn't have enough proof. We debated it for weeks—things became heated at times. They wanted me to go back to Poe again, to get indisputable evidence. I was concerned about going back a third time, given that we'd already altered history with our prior two jumps—even if it was just slightly. I didn't want to go again, but I had to try and figure out why only my interaction with Edgar Allan Poe seemed to alter our timeline."

"What did you end up doing?"

"We ultimately decided to go back, for one final visit."

Chapter 9
A Secret Worth Sharing

My sessions with Ethan had gone far better than I'd ever imagined they would. For the first time in ten years, I had begun to tell someone, outside the confines of Eastern State Hospital, my story—all of it. Regardless of whether he believed me or not, retelling the events that transpired before I'd committed myself had been remarkably therapeutic.

I'd told my story to both Alex and Dr. Monroe, but never experienced the same reaction I felt from talking with Ethan.

Employees at Eastern expected to hear stories like mine from residents. To them, I was one of many patients in a mental hospital. I was damaged, in some way, and my mind spun wild tales that I couldn't distinguish from reality.

Their job was to provide care for me. But for the ten years I remained in their care, I'd never expected them to believe me. I'd never expected to get well, because I didn't believe I was ill. Most of the non-residents at Eastern, whether they were staff or visitors, had a way of looking at patients that made us feel like something other than an actual person. They didn't see what I saw in my fellow patients. I saw people who happened to be ill, who wanted to be treated like everyone else. They deserved it as much as anyone did.

Conversations with Ethan were completely different. I knew he didn't believe me—at least for the first few sessions. He didn't even want to talk with me in the beginning. But that changed. He began to see me as a human being. He felt empathy for me. I'd even gotten the impression he was rooting for me, which had made me anxious about telling the rest of the story.

I was beginning to feel worthy myself. Perhaps enough to be forgiven for what I'd done. Perhaps I didn't need to stay at Eastern for the rest of my life. And though what happened to Poe was ultimately my doing, maybe it wasn't my fault—at least not mine alone. Maybe I'd suffered long enough for my part.

"Tristan, your father's out front. He's waiting for you," Alex announced.

"Perfect. I have something to tell him that might actually make his trip down here worth it."

"He's your father, T. It's always gonna be worth it to come down here and spend time with you."

"Well, my friend, perhaps he won't have to drive three hours to see me for much longer."

"What do mean, T? You planning a jail break?" my friend asked with a laugh.

"I don't know for sure—at least not yet. And that's just between you and me, okay?"

Alex's smile disappeared and his expression became blank. He nearly stumbled while turning to allow me to pass him on my way to the meeting room. I couldn't tell if he looked worried or sad. He actually looked a little like he was about to vomit. Perhaps he realized I wasn't kidding.

"Don't be sad, Alex. You're my friend. You'll always be my friend. I'll make time for you on the outside, if I ever actually decide to go."

My father looked at his watch and smiled as I entered the meeting room.

"I just got here. Alex must have made a strong case this time."

"He's a man of many talents," I answered with a smile.

"You look good, Tristan. If I didn't know any better, I'd suspect you're in a good mood. Been a while since I've seen a smile on my son's face."

"Dad, I have something to tell you," I announced in an effort to eliminate the small talk. This was going to be a serious conversation, and I wanted to set the mood.

"What's going on?" my father asked, bracing himself for something sarcastic, or cruel.

I wasted no time once I had his focused attention. "I'm still not completely sure, but I think I'm ready to leave this place."

My father froze. He pulled his bottom lip into his mouth and then let it out and swallowed. Tears began to build in his eyes, and he looked away as if he was afraid I'd noticed a moment of weakness.

He finally spoke, though I could barely understand his shaky words. "That'd be real nice."

"Now before you get too excited, and before you go and tell Mom, please remember what I just said. I'm still not completely sure. I need a few weeks to make my decision."

"Take your time, son. Just don't wait another ten years."

"I promise, I won't."

"Please tell me you're not playing some cruel game with me. Is this real?" my father asked.

I gave him another smile. "It's real. And I need to ask for a couple of favors, if you wouldn't mind."

"Anything."

"You'd mentioned last week that I could come and stay with you and Mom. If I do decide to leave, can I take you up on that offer? At least until I sort things out and get my life in order."

"We'd be thrilled to have you—for as long as you need, Tristan. Just come home," my father managed to add before a tear slipped down his cheek, and he turned his face away to hide it.

While my father wiped away his tears and gathered his composure, I set my copy of Ethan's book on the table and slid it over to him.

Before I came to Eastern, I'd managed to gather all of my notes on time travel, including the story about Edgar Allan Poe, and put them in a small metal box. My work—my accomplishments—were no longer under my control, and the Department of Defense would never share my discovery with the world.

I'd debated in my own mind for years whether time travel was best kept a secret, due to the potential dangers, before deciding to share this information with anyone.

When I'd determined I needed to share what I knew, I couldn't think of a better scientist to give my secret to than my father. He was a good man—he had a strong military background, so he understood the importance of keeping dangerous secrets. He was also a terrific scientist, so he'd know how to read my equations. He was a safe choice. Once he understood the science was real, he'd come around on the story about Poe. Maybe he'd even come to terms with my reasons for being at Eastern.

I had no doubt that my father was the only person I could share my notes with, should I not make it out of Eastern alive. And though it had been ten years, and I didn't think anyone would believe Ethan's article, I knew its looming release put my life at risk. My father would make an excellent insurance policy. My work, and my story, would not die with me.

He looked down at the copy of Ethan's book, and then to me with a furrowed brow.

I'd marked the letters inside the book, the same way he used to mark my books when I was a teenager— with a code to identify the location of my hidden notes. And I used the same location to hide my notes that he'd used for the last treasure he left for me, before I went off to MIT—a copy of *Gravitation*, a physics book on Einstein's theory of gravity, by Charles W. Misner, Kip S. Thorne, and John Archibald Wheeler.

The small metal box that contained my notes was buried just off a trail in Leakin Park, in Baltimore. I was sure he'd have no trouble finding it, nor discovering the code in the book.

"The second favor, Dad—read this when you get home."

He lifted his palms and shrugged, but I stopped him before he spoke.

"Promise me you'll read this book."

"Okay, I promise. I'll get to it during summer break, in a few weeks. And for now, I'm not saying anything about this to your mother."

He paused and put his hand on my shoulder. "This was a very nice visit, Tristan."

Chapter 10
Eureka!

I'd waited my turn in line, to be served breakfast, and exhaled loudly. And though I'd failed to hide my disdain, I managed to avoid shaking my head in utter contempt. Another Friday at Eastern. Another Pancake Day.

"Thank you," I managed with a weak smile.

My attention was immediately drawn to someone shouting my name from across the room.

"Tristan! Come sit next to me. I saved you a seat today," my fellow patient and friend, Max, called out across the cafeteria. He wore a smile that proved to be irresistible.

"That's nice of you, Max. Thank you. I'd be happy to sit with you," I replied, even though we'd sat at the same assigned table for years.

"I love Friday. I love pancakes," Max proclaimed melodically, tilting his head back and forth while adding another hefty forkful to his already overflowing mouth.

I returned the smile with a nod, and spread my napkin carefully on my lap. Time to enjoy yet another Pancake Day.

"Tristan, I love you. I love you the most. I don't want you to leave Eastern. I want you to stay here."

"Thank you, Max. And I love you right back. You're a good friend," I added.

I stopped for a moment, and stared at Max, waiting for him to elaborate. But he couldn't be dissuaded from his next bite.

"Max, who said I was leaving? There's been no announcement. At least none from me."

"Alex! Alex says you're not gonna be around. He says you're not gonna be around here much longer. I told him I didn't want you to leave. I don't want you to leave. I saved you a seat to tell you that."

"I'll have to have a chat with Alex. Don't be concerned, Max. I promise to talk with you before I make any decision to leave, okay?"

I'd searched for Alex both in and outside the building, but didn't find him before it was time to meet with Ethan. I'd have to answer a lot of questions now, and not just from my friends like Max. And I hadn't made any final decisions. I needed to ask Alex to stop talking about my potential departure, immediately.

I met Ethan outside while searching for Alex. "Hello, Mr. Alstead. Allow me to walk you in?"

"Good morning, Mr. Weare. Please, show me the way."

Once Ethan was properly signed in, I escorted him to the meeting room for our fifth session.

"The last time we spoke, you'd mentioned your apprehension for going back to visit with Poe a third time. But you ultimately decided to go ahead. What happened next?"

"Correct. While I was worried about the fact that we were actually altering history on our current timeline, I had to figure out why. The changes to Poe's literature had contradicted my theories, while other events, like the markers and military visits did not. I was determined to gather more data, and possibly revise my theories, if necessary."

"So you went back again?" Ethan asked.

"Yes. My security companion and I made a third jump—this time to Fordham, NY in 1847. Fordham is known today as the Bronx, but in Poe's time, Fordham was much more of a rural setting than it is today. Poe had leased a cottage in Fordham for the benefit of his very ill wife. In Poe's time, it was believed that fresh air could help with tuberculosis—even cure it."

"They were wrong," Ethan added.

"Correct again. Virginia died in January of 1847. The Edgar Allan Poe I met with, in the same cottage his beloved wife had passed months earlier, was not the same person I had met with before. He was devastated by the loss of his wife. His demeanor was different. His look had changed. He was in pain."

"What was your plan this time? Was he working on anything at all, while grieving the loss of his wife?"

"Some of his best work was actually written in that cottage—*The Bells,* and *Annabel Lee,* which was Poe's last complete poem. *Anabel Lee* was about the untimely death of a beautiful women. Many believe it was inspired by the loss of his wife. I happen to agree with them."

"Did you try to influence Poe's writing again, during this third visit?"

"I did, indeed. We knew at the Department of Defense that during the time of my third visit Poe was working on a book that happened to be in line with my specific area of expertise. It was a forty-thousand word prose poem about the origin of the universe that he published in 1848 titled *Eureka.* We planned the visit accordingly. With this cosmogony, I knew I had the perfect opportunity to add just enough current scientific theory to provide indisputable proof that I was there, with Poe, while he wrote it. I'd, of course, be careful enough to make it appear like just another *extraordinary coincidence* to anyone outside of the DoD."

"I'm familiar with *Eureka*. What parts did you influence? How did you know your superiors wouldn't also just dismiss another coincidence?"

"*Eureka* contains a detailed description of one of modern science's most famous theories."

I waited for Ethan to name it, but he just opened his eyes wider and tilted his head, slightly.

"The Big Bang Theory!" I shouted, startling my young friend.

"I described the origin of the universe, as widely accepted, in our current time. I gave Poe the perfect amount of detail to write about a theory that wouldn't be extensively discussed, or accepted, until about eighty years later. I gave him just enough information to intelligently put forth the idea, and describe it in a way that made sense to his readers. Of course, scientists in Poe's day dismissed *Eureka*. And so did the literary community. After its initial printing of five hundred copies, it wasn't reprinted for more than a hundred years. Until the start of the twenty-first century, *Eureka* was Poe's most ignored work."

"Was this enough to satisfy your bosses? Did your plan work?" Ethan asked.

"Yes, it worked," I answered softly, unable to look Ethan in the eyes. The excitement I had shown before vanished and I was overcome with sadness.

"This was the beginning of the end, wasn't it?"

"I'm afraid it was. When my companion and I returned to our current time, and back to our home office in Pottsville, PA, things quickly began to change. Once again, our markers in the Bronx weren't there, on our current timeline. Once again, no one at any of the military installations we'd visited in the past knew who we were. But Poe's work had changed. This time our evidence was accepted. My colleagues were ecstatic."

"What happened? How did you end up here?" Ethan inquired with enthusiasm.

"You're jumping ahead," I declared.

Ethan just shrugged, and motioned for me to continue.

"I'll get there in due time," I promised. "I was urged to take some time off—a long vacation, as a reward. I intended to use the time to revise my theory, due to the fact that I had actually changed history on my own timeline—something I'd theorized to be mathematically impossible before."

"They sent you on a vacation? After acknowledging you'd accomplished something that science had been dreaming about and chasing after for centuries? You should have been named a hero!"

"Much of the work we completed at the Department of Defense was kept under wraps. Our job was to make the impossible possible. And we didn't get much credit, or attention, for doing our job."

"How could you function that way? You traveled in time, and no one outside of your office believed it!" Ethan empathized.

"At the time I was more focused on understanding why I'd had an impact on my own history by traveling to the past. I spent the next several days at home, alone, revising my theory. I didn't want to celebrate, or be celebrated. I'd just been proven wrong."

Ethan shook his head, and closed his eyes. "What did you come up with?"

I looked at the clock and noticed our time was up. I didn't want to be interrupted by an orderly telling Ethan it was time to go. "That, my friend, is something we'll have to discuss next week."

Brian D. Campbell

Chapter 11
Are You Comfortable Here?

A routine can help manage stress. At least that's what Dr. Monroe said, constantly. He wasn't wrong. There are several important health benefits to keeping a regular routine—proper sleep habits, proper eating habits, healthy physical conditioning, and, of course, reduced stress levels.

We had worked out a regular routine for me, which included Pancake Day, Movie Night, arts and crafts, athletics, and other activities shared with my fellow patients. We'd also mixed in things I was allowed to do on my own, like gardening and reading.

The only problem with all this effort to avoid stress—there was nothing to be stressed about at Eastern. After ten years in an institution, the thing I believe I'd missed the most, was stress.

On Mondays, at two o'clock, my routine included a meeting with Dr. Monroe. Normally a psychiatrist and their patient in a mental health institution discussed a plan to help the patient learn to cope with life outside the institution. But that topic never came up during my weekly meetings with Dr. Monroe.

"Tristan, please come in. Sit down," Dr. Monroe requested when I arrived at his office, unescorted.

"Good afternoon, Doctor."

"I understand you have another visitor coming to see you weekly. This is an extensive interview—eight weeks, if I'm not mistaken. I thought they were done bothering you years ago. What's this one hoping to accomplish?"

"This one's no different than all the rest. Except for an extreme case of tardiness, I'd expect more of the same—a disappointing story that no one will bother to read," I lied.

"Why so many visits then, Tristan? Surely he could gather there's no story here in less time."

"I suppose my new friend from *Temporal Magazine* is a bit different, in some ways. He's far more patient— like a hunter, really. Not to worry. His persistence won't cause much of a stir. Our secrets are quite safe."

"We don't have any secrets at Eastern, Tristan. You're free to talk with your visitors about any topic you choose. I'd request that you keep our conversations in this room private, but otherwise your truth is yours to tell. We're not keeping you locked away from the outside. We only care about your treatment and wellbeing."

I nodded and smiled. I nearly chuckled.

Dr. Monroe leaned toward me, with his elbows on his desk and his hands together with his fingers intertwined. "Tell me Tristan, are you comfortable here?"

I was still thinking about the words Dr. Monroe so eloquently spoke, about his concern for my treatment and wellbeing. If there was a treatment plan for me, I wasn't made aware of it.

"I'm perfectly content, Doctor," I lied again.

"Excellent. That makes me happy to hear. The comfort of our long-term residents is one of my biggest concerns."

I couldn't help myself this time, and let out a laugh that I quickly tried to camouflage with a forced cough.

Once I was able to contain myself, I asked Dr. Monroe a question to lighten the mood. "Tell me, Doctor, are my friends at the Department of Defense still donating large sums of money to Eastern to ensure my care is as comfortable as possible?"

"We get many donations from government, as well as private organizations. Funding has never been a concern here at Eastern—we've managed to serve the community for a quarter of a millennium."

"Of course, Dr. Monroe," I replied. I wondered if we'd discuss my prognosis during this meeting. Or ever.

I'd left Dr. Monroe's office well short of the hour allotted to discuss my so-called treatment. And that was how our meetings progressed over the years. The major focus being placed on my comfort at Eastern, and little more. I wondered if one day we'd skip the meetings entirely. They'd become nothing more than a formality.

I'd decided to spend the rest of the afternoon, until dinner, working in the garden, alone, but my friend Alex came out to see me during one of his many smoke breaks.

"What's up, T? Been a few days, man. How was your meeting with Dr. M?"

"Uneventful, like the last four hundred and sixteen. At least we pretended for the first couple of years."

"I hear ya, man. Hang in there. Dr. Monroe isn't all that bad."

I just smiled.

"Did you tell him you were leaving?"

"No. And that's something we need to discuss, actually. I'd appreciate it if you'd stop telling the other patients that I'm going somewhere. I haven't made that decision yet, and when I do, I'd like to be the one to tell people."

"I don't know, T. You seemed pretty sure of it when we talked. You sure you haven't made up your mind?"

"I'm positive."

"I'd hoped I could talk you out of it. I'm worried about you, Tristan."

The fact that Alex addressed me by my actual name meant he was truly concerned. But why?

I stopped pulling weeds from the soil and stood, focusing my full attention on Alex. "I'm confused about something. Why do you seem so determined to talk me out of leaving here? We're friends, right?"

"Of course we're friends. How can you ask me that after all these years?"

"As my friend, I'd expect you to want what's best for me. I'm beginning to believe, for the first time in ten years, that I may not actually deserve to spend the rest of my life in this place."

Alex was no longer smiling, or joking, which was extremely unusual for him. In fact, until I'd told him about my potential exit from Eastern, I didn't think he was ever serious about anything. At least not while in my presence.

"I only want what's best for you, man. I promise you that." Alex had tears in his eyes.

I was surprised by the show of emotion from my friend. I didn't know what to say anymore, so I went back to the garden.

Alex began to walk away, and I stopped him. "Please just stop talking to others about me leaving. Okay?"

Alex didn't turn back to face me. He just kept walking. He acknowledged my request by raising his right hand in the air as he went back inside.

Chapter 12
Probable Reality

My good friend, Alex, had avoided me for the rest of the week after our talk in the garden on Monday. The chatter about my possibly leaving Eastern had stopped, so I assumed he did as I asked and stopped talking about it with others. But it seemed he'd stopped talking to me in the process.

I'd hoped to join him for a cup of coffee in the staff lounge Friday morning, before my sixth session with Ethan, but he was nowhere to be found. I was determined to resolve whatever issue he was having about my leaving, but I needed to understand it first.

I couldn't imagine he was just worried about losing a friend. But if it was indeed that simple, I wanted to assure him that he and I would remain friends outside the walls of Eastern State Hospital, if I decided to leave at all.

When one of the other orderlies tracked me down to tell me Ethan was waiting for me in the meeting room, I assumed Alex was possibly not at work at all that day. Maybe he'd been home sick all week, and I was making more of the situation than was necessary.

"Hello, Ethan. Good to see you again."

Ethan stood and shook my hand. "Good to see you too," he replied. "You know, I have to admit, I'm really into your story. I had my concerns in the beginning, but this is great stuff. I can't wait to put this thing together and give it to my editor."

"I'm glad you're coming around," I said, but I already knew his enthusiasm was growing based on the way he'd been reacting in our sessions. He was right. This was *great stuff*.

"We left off with you being sent on a little vacation last time. I also got the sense that when you got back to work, that's when everything went sideways," Ethan proclaimed.

"Yes, indeed. You can certainly say it went sideways from that point."

"Excellent. Well, I mean. Please continue from there."

I gave my young friend a smile to declare I wasn't offended. "Before returning to work, I'd made a modification to my theory about time travel. I still believed, as I do now, there are infinite-alternate realities which split from every timeline when something different actually occurs, or could occur. And when we go back in time to an alternate timeline and make a change, we'll most likely never see that change when we return to our own timeline. But we eventually proved, in our jumps to Poe's time, that some changes did make it back with us. That's where I made my modification. I believe we can logically assume not every possible outcome actually occurs, and it's quite logical that only the probable outcomes occur. Furthermore, if you make a change that also changes probable outcomes, it may alter a majority of alternate timelines."

"I don't get it," Ethan admitted.

"If you travel back in time and make a change on any timeline that makes the next series of events far more probable than they were before, you can alter the reality of most of the other timelines. Thus, you affect your own timeline, along with the majority of alternate timelines."

Ethan stared blankly.

"When I gave Poe the news story about Richard Parker, and the basics of the Big Bang Theory, it became highly probable that he'd use them in his writing. And he did, in almost all of the timelines from that point forward. We altered our own history based on probability. And thus, all of our visits with Poe from that point forward that resulted in a change became reality across all, or at least most, timelines."

"But what about the poem?" Ethan asked. He began riffling through his notes. "*Epigram for Wall Street!* That doesn't seem like something Edgar Allan Poe was highly likely to write. He didn't even put his name to it. How did that make it to our timeline?"

"Well done, Mr. Alstead. I'd considered the same thing. That's why I believe once we expanded the probability Poe would react to my visits, by giving him the irresistible Richard Parker story first, it became more likely that all of our visits would affect most timelines. If that's not the case, the only logical explanation about the poem is the same one my superiors came to ten years ago."

"An extraordinary coincidence?" Ethan asked.

"Indeed."

"So does that mean there aren't actually an infinite number of realities then? Since only the probable happens?"

"Of course not. There are an infinite number of *probable* realities to consider. It's just the most likely will occur many, many more times."

Ethan raised his brows and remained silent.

"Let me offer an example. While it's possible that every member of a certain species could wake up one morning and be infertile—meaning that species disappears when the current generation dies off, it's also extremely unlikely to happen. So, it doesn't. Thus the absurd, or improbable never happens, on any timeline. The same reasoning points out that when something is highly probable, it repeats itself on many, sometimes all, timelines."

Ethan smiled. "How do we know that's not what happened to the dinosaurs?"

"No. That's not at all what happened…"

"I'm only kidding," Ethan interrupted and laughed.

"Of course. Very funny."

"So, what happened when you went back to work? How did things begin to unravel?"

I took a deep breath, avoided the intense urge to explain the most likely cause of the dinosaur extinction in detail, and answered, "No one would look me in the eyes. People avoided me. No one wanted to be the first to tell me what happened while I was gone."

"What happened?"

"They jumped while I was away, without me," I said, feeling the same disbelief I had felt ten years prior. "And they went back to Poe again."

"Why would they do that?"

"A question I asked multiple people, multiple times," I answered. "And no one ever gave me any answers. Most of them denied knowledge that it had even occurred. But I knew it did when I inspected my equipment."

Ethan leaned in, put his elbow on the table, and rested his cheek on his open palm. He waited for me to continue.

"It seemed I'd lost control of the program. And no one had the courage, or the decency, to inform me officially."

"But why? What did they think you did wrong?"

"Perhaps it wasn't anything I'd done wrong at all. Perhaps I'd done everything right. And, as a result, my services were no longer required, at least not on that project."

"You just started working on something else then?"

"I'd expected to, at least. But I wasn't given any new assignments."

Ethan sat up straight, then leaned back in his chair, and finally raised his palms, "What the heck did you do next?"

"I had some free time on my hands," I answered softly. "So I decided to gather all of the current works published by Poe, and look for abnormalities, based on the jump my team denied knowing about."

Ethan's eyes widened. "What did you find out?"

I swallowed hard and answered, "A few things had indeed changed. In the current timeline that you and I are living now, Edgar Allan Poe had dreamed of one day creating his own periodical. He even had a name for it—*The Stylus.*"

"*The Stylus?* I've never heard of that."

"That's because it was never created," I answered. I still couldn't believe it was true and the words were difficult to say. I waited a moment, composed myself and continued. "However, before I'd left for my *little vacation,* Poe's dream was a reality. And, he'd published many of his most celebrated works in *The Stylus.* That magazine was real."

"But Poe died young, and in poverty. He never published any magazine…"

Ethan was interrupted by the same orderly that informed me he'd arrived an hour earlier. "Mr. Alstead, I'm afraid your scheduled hour is up."

Chapter 13
My Only Friend

For the first time in ten years, I'd managed to be in the meeting room before my father arrived for his weekly visit. I didn't wait for Alex to coax me out of my room, and then delay even further—first, because Alex seemed to be avoiding me, and second, to my astonishment, I really wanted to see my father.

"This is a wonderful surprise. It's great to see you, son."

I ignored my father's outreached hand, and nearly knocked his rigid body over with a hug. A handshake didn't feel appropriate.

"Your mother wouldn't believe me if I told her about that hug," he said, though I think he was grateful to be done with it. "She'd insist on coming with me next week, though. Do you think that would be okay?"

"Of course. It's been too long."

My father looked at me with an expression I'd never seen before. He looked proud. You'd think I'd have seen that look before, perhaps when I received my PhD from MIT, or a job offer from the Department of Defense to run their Physics Department. No. The first time I got the sense that my father was proud of me was at Eastern State Hospital—where I was a resident.

"Dad, have you read the book yet?"

"Book? Which book?"

I hadn't brought up Ethan's book for a couple of weeks, but it was summertime, and he'd promised to read it at the end of the school year. I needed to know he'd found the notes about my work and my experiences with time travel. I couldn't possibly bring that up at Eastern, in case someone was listening. I'd always felt like someone was listening at Eastern.

My expression turned to the much more stone-faced look I'm sure my father had become accustomed to. "The book I gave you a few weeks ago. The one you promised me you would read when school was out for the summer."

"Tristan, we just finished exams. I haven't even turned in my kids' final grades yet. I have the book. I'll get to it."

"Perfect, Dad. Why don't you come back when you've actually looked at it?"

The smile quickly vanished from my father's face, but he wasn't quite ready to give up on the visit that easily.

"Have you given more thought about coming home?"

I wanted to tell him yes, but hesitated and replied coolly, "No more thought than you've given to reading the book."

"I'll read the book, son. I promise. I'll start it when I'm done grading finals. I didn't realize it was that important to you."

I got up and walked to the door of the meeting room. "We'll talk when you're done reading," I said, and walked out, leaving my father there alone.

I wasn't sure why I did that to my father. Or why I'd done the same to him for ten years. This was, however, the first time I'd ever felt guilty about treating him unfairly. I needed a friend—a good friend.

I found Alex in the hall near my room and stopped him. "Alex, can we talk?"

"Um, sure, T. You doing all right? Should I let Dr. Monroe know you need some time with him?"

Alex had been back at work for several days, but our conversations were completely impersonal since he'd returned. It seemed as though our friendship had been reduced to nothing more than a patient-caregiver association. He was short with me—to the point. He never said anything more than what was required to do his job. I was determined to fix that, and this seemed like the proper time. I needed a friend.

"No, Alex. I want to talk with you," I insisted. "Alone."

"Let's take a walk outside, T."

I followed Alex out of the building. He didn't say a single word, and kept looking around as we walked to the doors.

"What's going on?" I asked. "You seem like you're on some secret mission lately."

"It's not like that. I'm worried about you, all right? You got it in your head that you need to leave here. I can't be any part of that. If someone thought I'd talked that notion into your head, I'd lose my job. I can't lose this job, T."

"How well do you know me? Do you think anyone here could ever talk me into doing anything I didn't want to do?"

Alex smiled and let out a laugh. "That's for sure, but not everyone around here knows you as well as I do."

"That's because you're my friend. And you'll always be my friend. Even after I leave this place—if I ever leave this place—whenever that may be."

"I think you're making a mistake, T."

"Then tell me about it, Alex. Explain why."

Alex didn't offer the explanation I'd requested. He looked at his watch and exhaled.

"I had an argument with my father. Over something stupid too. I think I actually feel guilty about it this time."

Alex gave me an expressionless look. "That's nothing new. You've run that poor man ragged for ten years. It's probably for the best that you finally feel bad about it," Alex hypothesized.

"And why is that, exactly?"

"Because maybe you'll start giving him the respect he deserves. He doesn't need to come out here and take your abuse week after week. But he does. And you keep giving it."

"I never really..."

Alex interrupted, "That's right. You *never really* nothin'!" He stopped, closed his eyes, and waved his hand—an apparent apology for raising his voice at me.

I nodded to indicate the apology was accepted.

"Look, don't sweat it, T. Your father will be back next week. Do the man a favor and remember the way you feel right now. Let that change the way you talk to him from now on. I gotta get back to work. Excuse me."

Alex walked back into the building and left me there, alone with my thoughts. I was at a loss for words. It seemed as though my friendship with Alex had expired at that point. Perhaps he was still hurting about the prospect of my leaving Eastern, or perhaps he'd had enough of my superiority complex. Either way, I felt as though I'd lost a friend—a good friend—my only friend.

Chapter 14
The Death of an Icon

The next few days at Eastern had been terribly lonely. Alex still wasn't speaking to me—at least not the way a friend would, and I was still upset about being rude to my father during his most recent visit. I attended all of my scheduled activities, and participated in good faith, but my spirits remained low.

I'd hoped an hour with Ethan, confessing my truth, would help improve my mood. I'd grown quite fond of him, and his increased enthusiasm at our weekly sessions was intoxicating.

I decided to surprise my young friend with a special treat that I wasn't sure he'd accept. At the very least, he'd be amused by the gesture and the atmosphere of our seventh session would be properly set.

"Good morning, Tristan. It's great to see you. What do you have there?"

"I'm sorry it took me so long to offer, Ethan, but better late than never, correct?"

"Pancakes?" Ethan asked, confused by the gesture.

"I've told you numerous times that Friday at Eastern is Pancake Day. And I'm dreadfully embarrassed that until now, I've never offered you a sample."

Ethan gave a hearty laugh. "Slide that plate over, my friend. I'd be honored to accept."

To my absolute delight, he devoured them. The mood had indeed been properly set.

Ethan quickly chewed and swallowed, favoring his sleeve over the napkin I'd provided him. "Last week you told me that you noticed Poe's history had changed, drastically, after someone used your equipment to travel back in time while you were away. I'd like for you to explain that in more detail," he added before draining the carton of milk I'd given him.

"There's a great deal to explain, I'm afraid, but I'll summarize," I offered. "First and foremost, *The Stylus*, along with many of Poe's most celebrated literary works, had ceased to exist. An American treasure was not just taken from us. It was obliterated from existence."

Ethan nodded while wiping milk from his lips with the back of his hand. "Yes, you'd mentioned that last time. What happened?"

"Mr. Poe's life ended twenty years prematurely, I'm afraid," I answered bluntly.

This caught my young friend by surprise. "Excuse me. Are you saying someone went back and killed him?"

"I can't say that, but I do know three things for certain. First, someone from my department made at least one jump to visit Edgar Allan Poe in 1849, while I was away. Second, Poe died in October of that same year. And third, before I'd left the DoD for a two-week vacation, Poe's history included achieving his lifelong dream of creating his own periodical, which he named *The Stylus,* and twenty more years of life."

Ethan stopped taking notes and leaned back in his chair with his arms crossed. "Well, damn. That's a whole lot to take in, isn't it?"

"Indeed," I answered. I waited for Ethan to digest the things I'd told him before I offered anything else.

"You don't know for sure if they killed him though, right?"

"As I said already. I can't say that."

"Can't, or won't?" Ethan persisted.

"Honestly, I don't even know for sure if Poe was murdered. I wasn't there, and none of my previous associates have ever admitted to me that they went back in time, let alone killed a man."

"I've done a little bit of homework," Ethan admitted. "There's all kinds of theories about the death of Poe. I'm now more interested than ever in your take."

"I thought you'd never ask," I said in a soft tone. "I don't know exactly how Mr. Poe died, but I believe he was murdered. And I've spent the last ten years feeling solely responsible."

"Because you invented the time machine," Ethan added.

I swallowed hard and responded, "Indeed. I invented a method for opening portals to alternate times and realities. Had I left Mr. Poe well enough alone, he would have achieved his dream of creating *The Stylus,* and lived twenty years longer."

"How do you believe Poe was murdered? What do you think happened?"

"Let's start with what you can read in history books, and go from there. In 1849, Poe was in Richmond, Virginia to give a few lectures and visit with old friends. He even proposed to Elmira Shelton, a woman with whom he'd shared a past relationship. But then he left, suddenly, telling friends he had to go to Philadelphia. However, he never actually made it to Philadelphia. In fact, no one knew where he was until he was found in an Irish Pub in Baltimore about a week after leaving Richmond, drunk and delirious, wearing a stranger's ill-fitting, shabby clothes."

"But he was alive when they found him?" Ethan asked.

"Barely. Over the next few days he slipped in and out of consciousness before passing out for the final time, and dying on October 7, 1849."

Ethan nodded. I'd supposed he'd done at least *a little bit* of homework.

I stopped for a moment to gain my composure, and continued, "Some believe the cause of death to be lesions on the brain, epilepsy, or even syphilis. There's a rather bizarre, but widely accepted theory that Mr. Poe was a victim of cooping—a common practice in Poe's time in which paid thugs would kidnap people, drug and disguise them, and then force them to vote, over and over at different polling places for specific corrupt candidates. There happened to be elections occurring the day he was found, and the Irish pub actually served as both a bar and a voting station."

"That's insane," Tristin said, before remembering where he was, and turning red.

"Indeed," I offered with a chuckle to help ease my friend's embarrassment.

"You don't believe any of those theories, do you?" Ethan asked.

"No, I don't. But I do have a theory of my own, and I'll share it with you, if you make me a promise."

Ethan furrowed his brow and leaned back. "A promise? What would you like me to do?"

"I can't prove anything I'm about to tell you. I no longer have access to any of the materials I'd need to do so," I admitted.

Ethan just stared at me with no expression.

"Remember when we first met? I told you that telling this story could put my life in danger."

Ethan flipped through his notes. "You said, 'There's an excellent chance that what I'm going to tell you could result in an untimely end to my life,' to be exact."

"Indeed. For your safety, I'd like for you to promise me that if you include what I'm about to tell you in your article, you make certain to document that you were shown no evidence to prove any of it."

"Of course. If that's the case, I'd be crazy not to," Ethan said, turning an even darker tone of red than before.

I laughed again. "Very well," I continued. "I believe someone from my group at the DoD visited with Poe, at least once, perhaps twice, and then poisoned him, in Baltimore. They picked that specific location, at that specific time, in order to create the speculation I just mentioned. Poe trusted them enough to be led into the trap, so I suspect my security companion, who possessed all of the skill and fortitude required to successfully complete such a mission, was one of the people who made the jump."

"That's a hell of an accusation. And you have no proof? Why didn't you gather evidence before you left the DoD?"

"It wasn't that simple," I replied, shaking my head. "I was experiencing an incredible amount of anguish upon learning that my equipment was used for murder—to murder someone I'd actually met, and idolized. I'd also begun to fear for my own life, given the circumstances."

"What were the circumstances?" Ethan asked.

"No one in my department would speak with me. My superiors hadn't given me any new assignments. I knew they'd made a jump in my absence, but no one would tell me anything about it. They acted as if they had no idea what I was even talking about—as if time travel were still a mere fantasy. When I finally broke down and told my supervisor everything, and asked him what he thought I should do, he suggested I come here and meet with Dr. Monroe. I did, and I haven't left here since—partly because I felt I deserved to be here for what I'd done, and partly because I feared if I left, I'd be murdered too."

Ethan looked down, and away. His eyes blinked twice and opened wider. Then he turned to me and asked, "Are you sure you have nothing at all to corroborate your story?"

Chapter 15
A Letter from a Friend

M y father hadn't missed a weekly visit in ten years. I felt horribly about how I'd spoken to him during our last visit and intended to apologize for it—and for the many years of torment I'd put him through.

I checked with the front desk, multiple times, but he never came. There were no messages for me either. My father had missed his first visit since I'd come to Eastern, and didn't call to let me know he wasn't coming.

In pain, I reached out to my friend Alex to talk about it, but he suggested I speak with Dr. Monroe instead. Alex was obviously still upset about my potential leaving.

Perhaps I should have listened to my good friend, who told me more times than I could remember that I should treat my father with more respect. Perhaps I should have done a great many things that I chose not to do.

In a lifelong effort to be less like my father, who could be cold and emotionless, it seemed I'd grown to be like him in every way. Our shared love of science never bothered me, in fact, it was our only bond. But my failure to treat those close to me with love and affection had never been more obvious to me.

I wasn't going to wait another week, hoping he'd show up, to apologize to him and make things right. And since I didn't have access to a phone, nor did I know his phone number, I decided to write my father a letter.

A simple apology wasn't enough, however. I had news to share as well. I'd made my final decision about leaving Eastern, and though I'd hoped to tell him in person, I didn't have that option at the moment. It had to be included to the letter.

I sat down in the Arts and Crafts Room with a pen and a stack of paper and wrote, while weeping like a small child.

Dearest Father,

Brian D. Campbell

I hope this letter finds you well. I missed you this week and I pray your uncommon absence wasn't the result of my terrible behavior.

I was cruel to you during your last visit. I'd been cruel to you during nearly all of your visits. For that I am deeply sorry.

I promise, the next time I see you, I'll be more cordial, and perhaps even shower you with the same affection I used to show Mom. Wouldn't that be a treat?

I'd also like to remind you, gently and respectfully, to please read the book I gave you a couple weeks ago. I'm anxious to talk with you about what you discover.

Last, and certainly not least, we spoke recently about my possibly coming home. I'd prefer to be telling you this in person, but I can't wait any longer to inform you of my decision.

Please tell Mom that I will be leaving Eastern State Hospital for good. Please hug her and kiss her for me, and tell her I'll be sure to do the same as quickly as possible.

I assume your offer to allow me to stay with you and Mom, for a short time, stands.

Your loving and appreciative son,

Tristan

After I'd finished the letter and regained my composure, I took it directly to the mailroom myself to be mailed. I was convinced that someone, other than its intended audience, would read it if I'd done otherwise.

When a clerk had finished helping with my outgoing letter, the office manager came bolting out of the mailroom with an enormous smile on her face.

"Hello, Tristan! It's kind of funny to see you here. I was going to have Alex bring this to you, but since you're here in person, here you go."

She handed me what appeared to be a very old, sealed package. I looked it over and discovered it was an envelope, sealed with wax.

"Where on Earth did this come from?" I asked.

"It's actually kind of an amazing story. That envelope was given to us in 1849, to be held for you and delivered ten years ago."

"And why am I receiving it now?" I asked, not yet considering from whom, and from when, this letter actually came.

"It was lost in the old building, in Williamsburg, for over a hundred years. The museum staff eventually found it and held onto it for a while, but then realized it was addressed to a current patient, over here, at the new, modern facility."

I stared at the envelope, stunned. Thoughts of what may be inside shook me.

"Isn't it amazing?" the office manager asked. "Look at the return address, Tristan!"

I picked up the envelope and examined it closer. The return address read only "Poe." And it was in fact addressed to me.

"Do you think that's from Edgar Allan Poe?" she asked, beaming.

I hardly looked at her, focusing on the envelope instead, and answered, "Don't be ridiculous. That's not possible."

Chapter 16
The Final Piece of Evidence

I resisted opening the envelope I'd received from the mailroom. For hours at a time, I stared at it. I inspected it fanatically, and ran my fingers over the red wax seal on the back. Perhaps I even hoped the wax would break under the weight of my fingers. Was there an actual letter from Edgar Allan Poe inside this envelope—addressed to me?

Ethan had expressed doubt during our last session together, asking me if I had any evidence at all to corroborate my story. Though I still wasn't certain of the contents of this mysterious envelope, we would open it together. Maybe we would discover the evidence Ethan was looking for.

I brought the envelope with me and waited patiently in the meeting room for Ethan to arrive for our eighth and final session together. I considered asking the office manager to join us for a part of the session, to confirm how this letter had come into my possession, but didn't feel that was necessary. Perhaps if there were questions, I could send for her later.

Ethan was finally led to the meeting room. "Good morning, Tristan. This is it, our final meeting. I'm excited to complete this project."

"As am I, though I'll miss spending an hour with you each week. It's been a pleasure."

"It's been interesting, Tristan. It's been extremely interesting."

Ethan set up his recorder and pulled his notebook and a pen out of his leather messenger bag. I laid the envelope on the table in front of me.

"What do you have there?" Ethan asked.

"This just came to me from the mailroom. I haven't opened it yet. I was hoping we could open it together, and solve that mystery."

"That just came to you? It looks like it's about a hundred years old."

"One hundred and seventy to be precise," I replied.

"Excuse me? What the heck is it, exactly?"

"I honestly don't know. I was told by the office manager that this envelope was hand delivered to the original structure that housed this institution in 1849, with instruction that it be delivered to me, ten years ago, which is when I first arrived here."

"You've been holding onto that thing for ten years?"

"No, I would have opened it immediately if I'd received it then," I answered. "I was told that the envelope was lost for over a century, and then rediscovered by museum staff at the old building in Williamsburg. One of them apparently looked at it more closely and realized it was addressed to me. They sent it over, and here it is—unopened for one hundred and seventy years."

"That's an amazing story, Tristan. Who's it from?"

I slid the envelope across the table so Ethan could read it.

"Poe? You've got to be kidding me!" he shouted. "Is this thing from Edgar Allan Poe?"

"I don't know. I haven't opened it yet. I have no idea what's inside," I admitted.

Tristan pulled out is cell phone and turned on his camera. "Do you mind?" he asked, before taking a picture.

I nodded in approval and he snapped several pictures of both sides of the envelope.

"We gotta open this thing," Ethan said with wide eyes and a huge smile.

I pulled it back and began breaking the wax seal.

"Careful, Tristan. Don't damage the contents," Ethan warned.

I gently pulled the envelope open, and discovered what appeared to be a letter inside.

"Open it carefully. It may be difficult to read."

I watched young Ethan contort his face several times as I unfolded the letter. He was even more excited than I was.

"Is it legible?" Ethan asked.

"Indeed it is," I answered and begun reading it aloud.

Richmond, September 26. 49.

My Dear Mr Weare

I have been visited today by two of your associates—one of them accompanied you during our three encounters over the last thirteen years. The other man wasn't you—which I found to be unusual. He didn't speak and seemed to be quite nervous—I suspect he was a security detail as he kept watch constantly—and rather nervously—over our surroundings. His name may have been Alex, but I can't be certain. I'm sure you know him.

Denying *The Stylus*

The encounter was unusual—as I stated. The man who I'd seen in previous encounters—when you were present—insisted that I travel to Baltimore, immediately. I'm not to tell a soul where I'm going—I suppose I shall tell my friends I'm leaving for Philadelphia, and I must leave at once.

I've been informed that you were placed in Eastern Lunatic Asylum and the purpose of my sudden travel to Baltimore is to aid in your release—somehow. I must admit I'm skeptical of this entire arrangement. I'm told that I may be to blame for your confinement and I'm terribly distressed. The people of your time have accused you of fraudulence—and a plan is afoot to prove otherwise. To that end—as I stated—I must travel to Baltimore at once.

My friend, I can't express how sorrowful I am to learn of your fate—but some part of me believes if I travel to Baltimore—I may meet a fate far worse. But I am not afraid. I have design of my own to exonerate you and I shall begin immediately.

I'm going to publish a periodical which I've named The Stylus—an ambition I've had for many years—In that periodical I shall educate the world of our encounters—directly. No one will ever doubt your honesty—or your integrity. This is my promise to you. If I should meet my end in Baltimore that will be tolerable. For meeting you has already proven to me that my words will never be forgotten. I have achieved immortality and informing me of this has been the greatest gift of friendship you could ever have given me. I hope these words—and those I intend to include in The Stylus—will change your fate and thus allow me to return as remarkable a gift as you've given to me.

Believe me your true friend.
E A Poe.

My heart sank and my eyes could hardly hold back the tears. I'd felt the guilt I first felt ten years earlier upon returning from my vacation to the Department of Defense. My discovery, and my actions, had led to the murder of Edgar Allan Poe—and the man considered me a friend.

Ethan sat across from me at the small table, silent for a moment, motionless. "Tristan, is that letter real?"

"I swear, the story I've told you about this letter is accurate. We can talk with the office manager, if she's available."

"No, don't bother. I know someone. Would it be possible to arrange a visit with a friend of mine? With your permission, I'd like to have her inspect this letter. She can authenticate it."

"Of course," I agreed quietly. "We can arrange that before you leave."

There wasn't much to say for the remainder of our hour together. We walked around campus, and Ethan took several pictures of me, the facility, and a few of the staff.

"Tristan, it has been amazing meeting with you. That letter! Oh my goodness, it's remarkable. I'll get my friend here within days, if we can. We have to authenticate that letter! It's incredibly important for the story."

I'd hoped to be more present during the moment, when it was time to say goodbye to Ethan. I'd planned to say a few words of encouragement and enthusiasm for his article, and express how fond I'd become of him during our eight sessions together. But my thoughts were in Baltimore—in 1849.

Chapter 17
A Moment to Clear the Air

T he letter I'd received from Poe nearly caused me to reverse my decision to leave Eastern. I'd begun to believe, again, that I deserved to spend the rest of my life locked away from the rest of the world and all of the people and things I loved.

But when I read it again, and again several times over the weekend after my final Friday session with Ethan, I noted that Poe knew his life was in danger. He'd suspected there could be peril waiting for him in Baltimore, but he still decided to go—because he'd been told I needed his help.

I'd considered the fact that Poe most likely didn't want me to waste away in an institution, even if our ill-fated meeting ultimately resulted in a tragic end to his life. He expressed gratitude for my confirming to him that his work would be remembered forever, while knowing his life was in danger.

I believed, strongly, that Edgar Allan Poe would want me to leave Eastern. So, I made the final decision to tell Dr. Monroe during our weekly meeting on Monday that I'd no longer be requiring his services, or remaining in his care.

As I made my way to Dr. Monroe's office, a half an hour early, my good friend Alex stopped me in the hall. I was happy to see him—I wanted to share the news.

"What's up, T? You got a minute, right? It's not time for your meeting with Dr. Monroe just yet."

He called me T. His familiar tone was nice to hear. Perhaps he'd finally gotten over his anger about my leaving. This couldn't have worked out better if I'd planned it.

"Come walk with me for a minute. I'll buy you a cup of coffee," Alex offered.

I smiled and accepted, "Alex, you know the world's worst coffee is served daily, for free, in the staff lounge. You don't have to pay for it. Perhaps they should pay us to drink it."

"Damn right, T. 'Bout time you figured that out too."

I followed Alex to the staff lounge and laughed to myself for trying to get to Dr. Monroe's office early. I'd made him wait weekly for ten years. Why change the pattern now, just because I intended to leave.

I noticed Alex was looking around, through the halls, and into each open door we passed. He seemed nervous—even a little twitchy.

"After you, my friend," Alex offered when we made it to the empty staff lounge.

And then he did something unusual. He looked both ways, down the hall, and locked the door to the staff lounge after he entered.

I started to ask him why he'd locked the door, but he spoke first. "We need to have a private conversation. It's been a while since we've talked. I wanna clear the air before it's too late."

"That sounds perfect," I replied.

I sat at a table and waited while Alex poured two cups of coffee and fixed them to our usual preferences. With his back turned to me, he spoke. "I understand you're going to be leaving us soon."

"Yes, I've made my decision. I am leaving. I intend to tell Dr. Monroe that in a few moments."

"It's a damn shame, T. I'm really gonna miss you."

"You know, Alex, I hate the way things have been between us recently. You're my friend. You're my only friend."

"Me too, buddy. That's why I wanted to have this talk with you, before you pack up and head on out of here, for good."

"This doesn't need to be the end of our friendship. I'll be in Baltimore, but that's only about a three hour drive from here. We could meet in the middle," I suggested. "Perhaps catch up over something a little stronger than a cup of terrible coffee?"

Alex laughed. "Let's talk about that in a minute," he replied as he handed me a cup and sat across from me.

I thanked him and began to take a sip.

"Wait, hold up, T. First, let me offer a toast."

I smiled and we raised our cups.

"To ten years of friendship."

We both drank and set our cups down on the table. It really was the world's most terrible coffee. I opened my eyes wide and blinked a couple of times. It seemed I was losing focus, and then I felt as if the room had begun to move in circles around me.

"Ten God-damned years of babysitting your sorry ass in this nut house," Alex added.

I tried to focus my attention on him, but I could hardly hold my head still.

"Don't sweat it, T. The poison I gave you is much stronger than what we gave Poe. It's not gonna take days to put you down. And ain't no one gonna know what caused your heart to explode in your chest."

I began to have trouble breathing and my chest felt tight. I pushed the coffee cup away, knocking it over.

"You already got more than you need, T. That's not gonna help you now."

I exhaled strongly and coughed. "You! You're the Alex from the letter."

He pulled Poe's folded letter out of his pocket and held it up, "You mean this letter, right here?"

I couldn't speak anymore and struggled to keep myself upright in my chair. I watched in horror as Alex carried Poe's letter over to the sink, and pulled a lighter out of his pocket. He wouldn't!

"You know, I might have let you go. I mean no one knows who you are anymore. Ain't nobody gonna believe that article in *Temporal*," Alex added, shaking his head. "Even though my instructions were to end your life if you ever tried to leave here. I might have let you go."

I fell to the floor, gasping for air. It felt like an elephant was stepping on my chest.

"But this damn letter," Alex continued, lighting the lighter under the bottom corner. "This letter is just too much to overlook."

He lit the letter and held it above the sink, until the flames began to touch his hand, and then he dropped it and let it burn out.

I could feel myself losing consciousness as the letter was engulfed in flames.

Alex stood over me, watching me die. "You know I hated it here at first. For years I was pissed off about being assigned to you. But then, after a while, it wasn't so bad. Hell, I actually did consider you a friend for the last couple of years. I wouldn't have minded spending the rest of my career hangin' out here, with you."

My throat closed completely, and the room grew darker.

Alex let out a forced chuckle. "Mad scientist! Huh. You know what my favorite part was about traveling through time? When you do something in the past that changes your own reality, and no one else even notices—except you. Talk about a power trip."

I laid there, motionless, powerless—slipping into darkness as I heard Alex's next few words.

"Don't worry so much, T. You'll probably get a chance to tell your story, eventually. Perhaps in an alternate reality."

Indeed.

Also By Brian D. Campbell

The Third King: Coronation
Part I of the Ben Gilsum Book Series
(Red Cliff Press, 2018)

Guardian Angel: True Calling
Part II of the Ben Gilsum Book Series
(Red Cliff Press, 2019)

For More Information

Visit our website:
www.redcliffpress.wordpress.com/